Bobbin Dustdobbin

A Richard Jackson Book

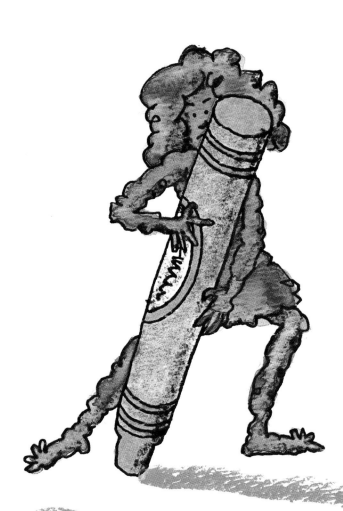

Bobbin Dustdobbin

Story by
Susan Patron

Pictures by
Mike Shenon

Orchard Books / New York

For my two daring nieces, Thérèse Tuttle
and Erin Chun—S.P.

For my father, Philip John Shenon—M.S.

Orchard Books
95 Madison Avenue
New York, NY 10016

Manufactured in the United States of America. Printed by Barton Press, Inc. Bound by Horowitz/
Rae. Book design by Mike Shenon. The text of this book is set in 16 point Caslon 540. The
illustrations are ink line and watercolor drawings reproduced in full color.

10 9 8 7 6 5 4 3 2 1

Library of Congress Cataloging-in-Publication Data
Patron, Susan. Bobbin Dustdobbin / story by Susan Patron ; pictures by Mike Shenon.   p.   cm.
"A Richard Jackson book."
Summary: Bobbin Dustdobbin, who lives in the dust under Billy Que's bed, fears for her safety
when five bad boys propose to sweep out Billy's house in honor of his birthday.
ISBN 0-531-05468-3.—ISBN 0-531-08618-6 (lib. bdg.)   [1. Fantasy.]
I. Shenon, Mike, ill.   II. Title.   PZ7.P27565Bo   1993   [E]—dc20   92-25099

Every morning, Bobbin Dustdobbin tumbled out of her Popsicle stick bed and rolled around on the floor to get herself a good thick coating of dust. Then she sniffed, snuffed, sneezed, and snorted, and the dust balls clung nicely to her, top to bottom. "Whoosh," said PapaHob, for he was proud of his dusty daughter.

Bobbin Dustdobbin was also wonderfully nosy. She took care of things close to the floor, so she knew about every leak, creak, drip, draft, crack, ant, spider, fly, hole, clog, rip, tear, breakage, and blockage in Billy Que's house. "Whoosh," said PapaHob, for he was mighty proud of his nosy, dusty daughter.

Mighty proud, except for one thing.

Bobbin, daughter of Hob, was not daring. At least, Hob thought not. No, not daring enough to learn Sizechanging, for it takes a stout heart to learn the useful Dustdobbin trick of changing the sizes of things.

One time, PapaHob had had to do a Sizechanging trick on Billy Que—he shrank him.
That trick taught Billy Que a lot about smallness,
meaning he became more careful and more kind.
And from then on Billy Que and PapaHob
Dustdobbin had no more squabbles—in fact,
they took to playing checkers and hobnobbing
together most evenings after supper.

But not Bobbin. She purely could not abide
Billy Que because he kept an old broom on his
porch, and Bobbin *hated* brooms. PapaHob didn't
mind it, since Billy Que had never actually *used*

the broom—never even touched it. But Bobbin was galled and vexed and just plain *mad* that he kept that broom at all.

So she kept her distance from Billy Que.

Also, she kept a secret from him.

It had to do with a house key, a lost house key, Billy Que's lost house key, missing so long that there was dust in the keyholes.

Bobbin knew where it was (behind the cookstove) because she knew *everything* that went on close to the floor. But she did not tell, and she did not return that key; nor *would* she return it as long as Billy Que kept that old broom on his porch.

So on this one particular day, when Billy Que
came looking for Hob, Bobbin went deep under
the bed, where he could not see her, glowering
fiercely among the dust balls.

Billy Que said, "Seeing as it's my birthday,
I put a cake in the oven to bake. You'd be
welcome to share it with me."

"Much obliged," said PapaHob, and went
along with Billy Que to the kitchen.

Now pretty soon the smell of that baking cake got into town, where five bad boys were doing their chores. Soon as they smelled that good cake-baking smell, they aimed to have some, so one after the other each boy dropped his mop

and his rag

and his brush

and his broom

and his sponge   and took off running.

The cake was cooling and Billy Que and Hob Dustdobbin were making the frosting when the five bad boys arrived, poking and choking and sparring and jarring.

Hob hid himself when the boys barged into the kitchen.

"We smelled your cake, Billy Que," said the first.

"And we want some!" said the second.

"With lots of frosting!" said the third.

"And ice cream!" said the fourth.

"Whoosh," said the fifth. "If it's your birthday, show us your presents!"

"Didn't get any," said Que, "'cept this here cake, which is my present to myself and which you boys are welcome to share. Presents don't matter none to me."

The five bad boys kicked their feet and
shoved one another with their shoulders. Then
one of them said, "We'll be back when you finish
getting that frosting on," and they ran around
the house. They crowded together on the back
porch.

Even bad boys know that presents *do* matter. Especially on your birthday.

"We ought to give old Billy Que a present," said the first.

"But we got no money," said the second.

"Make him something," said the third.

"Haven't got anything to make him something out of," said the fourth.

"Whoosh," said the fifth, who spied the old broom leaning against the house. "We could do Billy Que's chores for him."

The boys looked through the window. They did not see Bobbin Dustdobbin watching and listening and glowering.

"We could sweep in there," said one boy. "Shake out the rug, dust and scrub."

Bobbin was galled! Disturbing the dust where Dustdobbins live is a terrible thing to do. Those bad boys had to be stopped!

But on they went with their plan. "Let's go get birthday cake, then come back real quiet, few by few, and sweep up his room," they said. "Won't old Billy Que be surprised!"

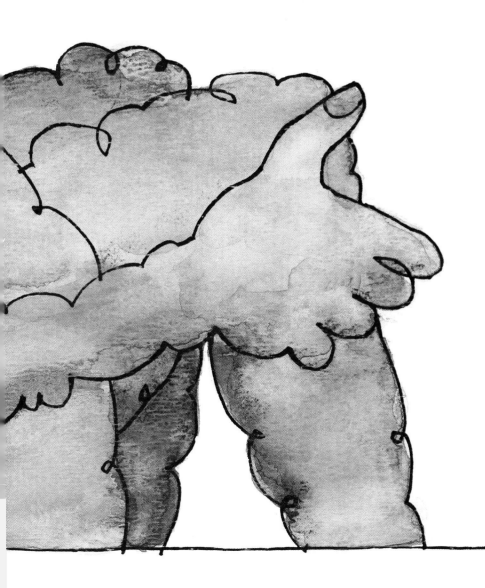

Just then Billy Que called,

"*Cake!*"

so those boys all ran back to the kitchen.
Bobbin saw her chance. She took her scissors
and ran out to the porch.

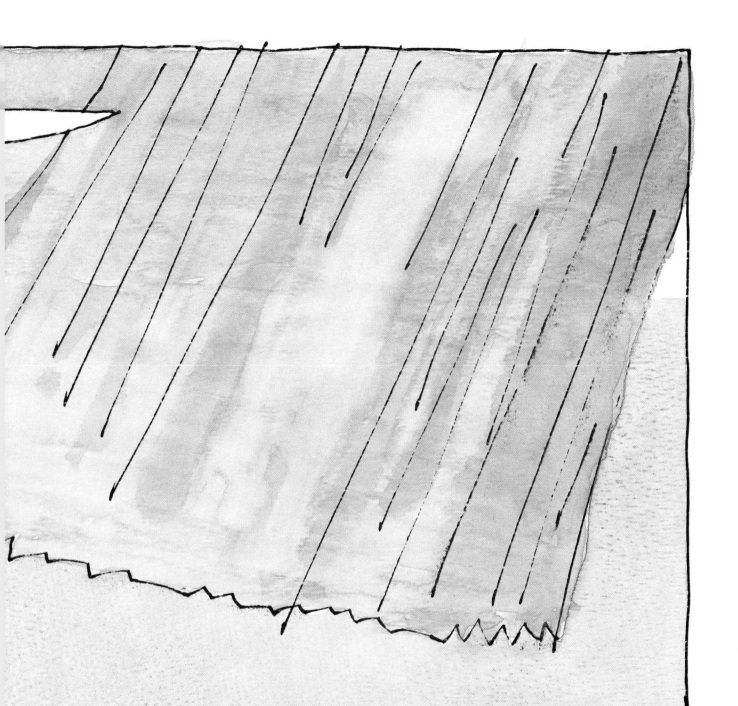

She snipped broomstraws off that broom, and
as she snipped she sang,

> "Snip, snip, scissors,
> snip, snip, cut.
> Off with all the broomstraws,
> no matter what!"

Then two boys came running back, licking their fingers, so Bobbin hid herself.

"Something's been snipping this broom!" said the one.

"Something sharp and swift!" said the other. Before they could think what to think, Billy Que called,

"Ice cream!"

so they ran back to the kitchen.

Bobbin came out again with her scissors
and cut more broomstraws, and as she snipped
she sang,

"Snip, snip, scissors,
snip, snip, cut.
Off with all the broomstraws,
no matter what!"

But then two more boys came running back, licking their fingers, so Bobbin hid herself.

"Something's been snipping this broom!" said the one.

"Something sharp and swift!" agreed the other. But before they could think what to think, Billy Que called,

"Seconds on cake and ice cream!"

so they ran back to the kitchen.

Bobbin came out with her scissors and cut off all the rest of the broomstraws, and as she cut she sang,

"Snip, snip, scissors,
snip, snip, cut.
Off with all the broomstraws,
no matter what!"

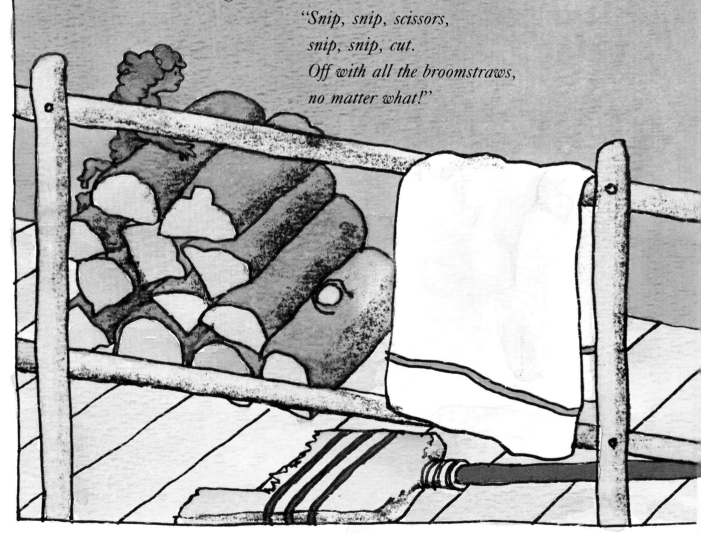

The instant she finished, the last boy came running, licking his fingers. Bobbin hid herself, too vexed to be much afraid. The boy saw the broom and the pile of broomstraws, and he hollered, "Billy Que, come quick! Something sharp and swift has cut your broom, and now there's nothing left of it!"

Billy Que came running, and also the other four boys, and also PapaHob (perched and hidden on Billy Que's hat) who right away saw his stouthearted daughter in her hidey-place.

"Better get you a new broom, Billy Que," said that boy. "This one here is worthless."

Que thought about that and scratched his head and seemed to look right at Bobbin where she sat hidden, though it's doubtful that he could have spotted her.

"Naw," he said. "I don't need me a new broom. I never did like to sweep."

So Billy Que, he got none of the wrapped-up
kind of presents for his birthday, but every
whisk, pot, pan, spatula, beater, bowl, and dish
in his kitchen got washed, wiped, and polished
by the five bad boys. He was right pleased, and
mighty flabbergasted.

And that night he discovered something on
the windowsill of his bedroom. It was a funny
little basket that looked to be woven from
broomstraws. In it was the house key he had lost
long ago.

And from then on *all* the small things he lost
turned up sooner or later in the broomstraw
basket.

Lnd dusty, nosy, *daring* Bobbin
Dustdobbin, stouthearted daughter of Hob,
began her Sizechanging lessons the very
next day.